O

I

MA

C

AFRICA DREAM

AFRICA DREAM

by Eloise Greenfield
illustrated by Carole Byard

The John Day Company
New York

I went all the way to Africa
In a dream one night
I crossed over the ocean
In a slow, smooth jump

And landed in Africa
Long-ago Africa

I went to the city
And shopped in the marketplace
For pearls and perfume

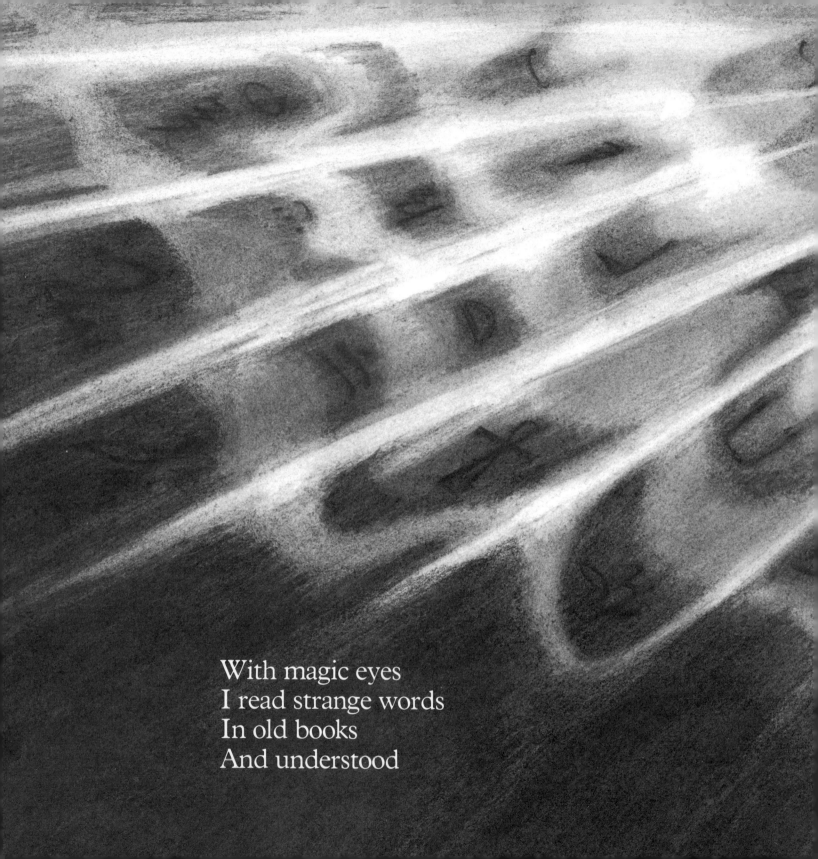

With magic eyes
I read strange words
In old books
And understood

I leaned small against
Tall stone buildings

And rode through the crowds
On a donkey's back

I dreamed I went to Africa
Long-ago Africa
I went to the village
And stood lonesome-still

Till my long-ago granddaddy
With my daddy's face
Stretched out his arms
And welcomed me home

He knelt on one knee
And planted one seed
That grew into ten tall trees
With mangoes for me

I danced a hello dance
To the drums of my uncles

And sang a hello song
In a circle with new-old friends

I walked with my cousins
All over Africa
Lifting my long dress
To step across countries

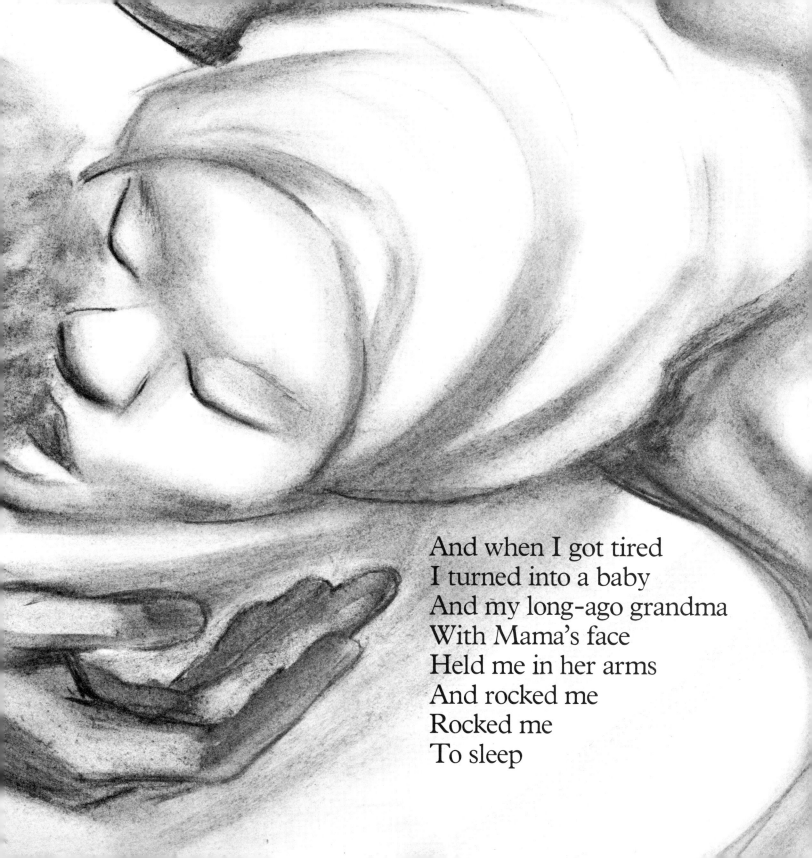

And when I got tired
I turned into a baby
And my long-ago grandma
With Mama's face
Held me in her arms
And rocked me
Rocked me
To sleep

Eloise Greenfield is the author of several books for children, and since 1965 her short stories and articles have appeared in *Black World, Ebony Jr!, Scholastic Scope,* and other magazines.

Ms. Greenfield's biography and fiction for children have received numerous awards, including the first Carter G. Woodson Award for her *Rosa Parks,* and the Jane Addams Children's Book Award for her *Paul Robeson.* She has received a citation from the Council on Interracial Books for Children in recognition of her "outstanding and exemplary contributions to...children's literature."

Carole Byard who also illustrated the Crowell Biography *Arthur Mitchell,* is a brilliant young painter whose first stay in Africa was on a grant from the Ford Foundation. Recently she made a second trip, to Nigeria, as a delegate to an international black arts conference. Her exciting pictures for *Africa Dream* reflect her loving study of African life and culture.